Camille loves to build sand forts at the beach. But it's hard to build a big fort alone. See what happens when Camille and her friends make a plan, work together, and share the fun.

Stuart J. Murphy

Camille's Team

Social Skills: Cooperation

Stuart J. Murphy's

I See I Learn

Charlesbridge

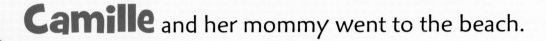

Camille and her mommy went to the beach.

Camille liked jumping in the waves.

She liked collecting shells.

And, most of all, she liked building forts in the sand.

Soon Carlos walked by.

"Hi, Camille," he said. "What are you building?"

"A great big fort," said Camille.

"I'm going to build a big fort, too," said Carlos.

Then Percy and Freda came along.
"What are you building?" asked Percy.
"A big fort," said Camille.
"Me, too," said Carlos.

"I'm going to build a fort, too," said Freda.
"And mine's going to be bigger than both of yours."

"Mine's going to be the biggest fort of all," said Percy.

Soon Carlos saw that his fort wasn't getting very big.

Freda's was so small that it didn't look much like a fort.

Percy's was still pretty small, too.

Then a big wave splashed up and washed everyone's forts away.

"What if we all work together?" said Camille. "That way we can build one really BIG fort." "Good idea," said Freda. "Let's **cooperate**."

"We can be the Big Fort Team,"
said Carlos.
"Cool," said Percy.

make a plan

Carlos filled his pail with sand.

Freda scooped with Camille's shovel.

Percy dug with his hands.

work together

As they piled the sand up,
Camille patted it down.

Carlos filled the pail with more sand to make towers.

Freda built some walls.

Percy dug a moat around the outside.

share the fun

"Go, team!" said Camille as she raked the sand.

They worked together.
The fort got bigger and bigger.
"Yay, team!" said Camille. "We're almost done."

Carlos found some sticks that looked like poles.

Freda stuck a big leaf on the top of each pole to make a flag.

Percy filled the moat with water.

cooperate

And Camille put shells
all around the walls.

It was such a big fort that everyone stopped to look.
"Who built that fort?" someone asked.
"The Big Fort Team!" said Camille.

"That's us!" they all shouted.

work together

share the fun

make a plan

cooperate

A Closer Look

1. How do **you** cooperate with others?

2. Look at the pictures.
   What happened when everyone started to work together?

3. How is working together better than working separately?

4. Work with a friend to draw a picture of a fort like the one Camille's team built.

A Note About Visual Learning and Young Children

Visual Learning describes how we gather and process information from illustrations, diagrams, graphs, symbols, photographs, icons, and other visual models. Long before children can read—or even speak many words—they are able to assimilate visual information with ease. By the time they reach pre-kindergarten age (3–5), they are accomplished visual learners.

I SEE I LEARN™ books build on this natural talent, using inset pictures, diagrams, and highlighted words to help reinforce lessons conveyed through simple stories. The series covers social, emotional, health and safety, and cognitive skills.

Camille's Team focuses on cooperation, a social skill. Learning how to work together to achieve a goal is essential, as it helps children develop mutual respect. Children see that they can get more done—and have more fun doing it.

Share the work. Share the fun!

Stuart

Photo © ArsAgassiz.com

Stuart J. Murphy is a Visual Learning specialist and the author of the award-winning MathStart series. He has also served as an author and consultant on a number of major educational programs. Stuart is a graduate of Rhode Island School of Design. He and his wife, Nancy, live in Boston, Massachusetts, near their children and three grandchildren, Jack, Madeleine, and Camille.

Published by Charlesbridge
85 Main Street
Watertown, MA 02472
(617) 926-0329
www.charlesbridge.com

Color separations by Chroma Graphics, Singapore
Printed and bound September 2010 by Jade Productions
in Heyuan, Guangdong, China

Library of Congress Cataloging-in-Publication Data
Murphy, Stuart J., 1942–
　　Camille's team / Stuart J. Murphy.
　　　　p. cm. — (An I see I learn book. Social learning/Cooperation)
　　Summary: At the beach four animal friends work together to make a fabulous sand fort.
　　ISBN 978-1-58089-458-6 (reinforced for library use)
　　ISBN 978-1-58089-459-3 (softcover)
　[1. Cooperativeness—Fiction. 2. Beaches—Fiction. 3. Animals—Fiction.]
　　I. Title. II. Series.
PZ7.M9563Cam 2011
[E]—dc22   2010007580

Printed in China
(hc)　10 9 8 7 6 5 4 3 2 1
(sc)　10 9 8 7 6 5 4 3 2 1

Stuart J. Murphy's

I See I Learn™

teaches important skills for school readiness and daily life:

- **Social Skills**
- **Emotional Skills**
- **Health and Safety Skills**
- **Cognitive Skills**

Each book includes **A Closer Look:** two pages of activities and questions for further exploration.

Stuart J. Murphy is a Visual Learning specialist and the acclaimed author of the award-winning MathStart series.

www.iseeilearn.com

Charlesbridge

85 Main Street
Watertown, MA 02472
(617) 926-0329
www.charlesbridge.com